THE RED LANTERN BAR AND GRILLE

PALMETTO
PUBLISHING
Charleston, SC
www.PalmettoPublishing.com

The Red Lantern Bar and Grille
Copyright © 2024 by Stanley N. Fulford

First Edition

Paperback ISBN: 9798822963498
eBook ISBN: 9798822963504

THE
RED
LANTERN
BAR AND
GRILLE

STANLEY N. FULFORD

CHAPTER 1

IT WAS 1997 IN THE PICTURESQUE BEACHSIDE TOWN OF
Mexico Beach, Florida. Located in the panhandle of the state,
it faces the Saint Joe Bay and is separated from the Gulf of
Mexico by Cape San Blas.

The small community was developed in the early 1960s by a
retired air force officer from San Diego, California, named Sam-
uel Halstead. He was a lieutenant colonel stationed at Tyndall Air
Force Base, which adjoins Mexico Beach. He believed the five-
mile stretch of pristine beach with its sugary white sand could
become a retirement community and popular tourist destination
because of its one-mile, unobstructed view of the Gulf of Mexico.
With mild temperatures and excellent spring and fall fishing, the
area made Halstead feel certain he could develop it. He had no
desire to return to his birthplace and retired in the nearby town
of Apalachicola in1957 along with his wife, Elsie.

The 1930s saw the completion of US Highway 98, which
increased the number of visitors to the area. In 1941, Tyndall

Field was built and became the training site for pilots in the air force. Growth was slow, and the sleepy beach town remained quiet.

By 1967, the little town was ready to incorporate, and the City of Mexico Beach was formed. Retired Lieutenant Colonel Halstead had purchased thirteen hundred acres on May 1, 1959, for the sum of $70,000 and was a major contributor to the development of the area. Sam and Elsie Halstead were excited to finally begin developing their property.

By 1997, Mexico Beach had grown to a population of twenty-five hundred permanent residents. The local chamber of commerce reported that during each of the years from 1994 through 1996, the number of tourists and fishermen swelled to just over ten thousand in each of the six months between May and October, thanks to the development efforts of Halstead years before.

Mexico Beach boasted several restaurants, a post office, a dozen mom-and-pop hotels, two locally owned grocery stores, a miniature golf course, a funeral home, an RV park, and a number of bait-and-tackle stores, along with several churches. Its continued future growth was a sure thing.

Greg and Jonathan Hughes were two brothers who had been born in the neighboring town of Panama City, Florida, located thirty miles west of Mexico Beach. This was the nearest city with a hospital, where nearly all the children in Mexico Beach had been born. Greg was now age thirty and John twenty-six.

Both brothers graduated from Florida State University in Tallahassee with business degrees, Greg with a BS in accounting and John a BS in marketing. Their parents encouraged them to pursue these degrees, believing they would provide them a foundation for developing a business or businesses in their hometown. Greg worked at the local CPA firm, where his dad was a partner. John worked as a marketing rep for a Mexico Beach real estate developer.

The two men had dreamed of opening a new restaurant in their hometown. Their parents had encouraged them to get their education and then pursue their shared goal.

The brothers were privy to the increasing numbers of tourists visiting the area via the chamber's report. There had not been a new restaurant opened in nine years. John identified a piece of undeveloped property on the beach side of Highway 98 and suggested to his brother that it would be the perfect location. The problem was the price. There was no way John and Greg could afford to buy it, much less develop it.

On July 4, 1995, their parents were tragically killed in an auto accident with a drunk driver who crossed into their lane, hitting them head-on and killing both instantly. The intoxicated driver was uninjured. Greg and John were the equal beneficiaries of the life insurance proceeds totaling $1 million. Additionally, the parents left their sons the family house, which was mortgage free.

The young men's parents had moved to Mexico Beach with plans to retire there. Their dad had been a successful

CPA and their mom a high school English teacher. The family was well known and respected by all. The community was greatly saddened by the loss of their two friends and fellow community leaders, and some wondered how the two young men would handle their sudden windfall.

The services were performed at the local funeral home owned by Stephen and Leticia Sadler. Stephen and Greg were the same age and had grown up together in the community. They both attended FSU, where Stephen had graduated with a BS in criminal justice, with concentrated studies in forensic science. His father had encouraged him to pursue the degree to better equip him for the future role of owning the funeral home. Stephen would also later be elected the county's coroner.

Greg, along with his wife, Sarah, and John, with his wife, Jessica (Jessie), put their parents to rest in the cemetery where the Hughes family owned plots.

CHAPTER 2

JOHN AND GREG'S PATERNAL GRANDPARENTS LIVED IN THE mountains close to the Nantahala River Gorge near Franklin, North Carolina. They were born there and had lived their entire lives in those mountains.

When the boys were young, they spent a week visiting their grandparents nearly every year. For the most part, they loved it, except when their grandfather got a snootful of mountain moonshine and transformed into an ornery old drunk. He would curse and yell at their grandmother, whom they loved dearly, and sometimes became physical with her if she didn't do as he said. The boys would hide in their bedroom until their grandfather passed out from his intoxication. They would then exit to check on their grandmother, who sometimes had bruises from his repeated slaps. They hated him when he behaved in this manner.

On one visit, the boy's grandparents attended a wedding of one of their friend's daughters down the mountain and took the boys along. Greg was fourteen and John ten. By the end of the ceremony, their grandfather had become drunk. Some of the attendees begged him not to drive home, even though it was only a few miles up the mountain. That evening, he ran off the road and hit a tree, killing his wife. He and the boys were spared from injury. The boys despised their grandfather for this senseless accident that could have easily been avoided.

A year passed. Greg and John returned for another week-long visit, except this time, it was without their beloved grandmother. Their grandfather had become angry with himself about the loss of his wife. He was now drinking every day, trying to numb the pain of his foolishness.

After their grandfather beat John with his bare hands over a simple mistake he had made in the sawmill, Greg became so angry he devised a plan to kill him. During a walk that crossed over a deep ravine to their favorite swimming hole, Greg was overcome by a fit of rage and pushed his grandfather to his death. The two brothers retrieved the body and brought it back to the sawmill, where they dismembered it, using the powerful blades used to cut logs.

They sawed off his arms and legs first, then his feet and hands, and finally his head. They shaved off the meaty parts of his body, wrapped them in the wrapping paper their grandmother had used to wrap slaughtered cows with and sold it to the local meat market as beef. They burned his head and pulverized the skull and all the bones using the press in the sawmill. They bagged the crushed bones and scattered them in various places across the mountain.

Greg called his father and explained everything the brothers had done. He told them to say nothing to anyone and that he was on his way. The sheriff arrived and asked the boys what happened. They explained that their grandfather got drunk (the sheriff was well aware of his alcoholism) and wandered off into the woods and didn't come back.

After searching the area for two days, the sheriff and his deputies turned up nothing…no trace of the man at all. The sheriff figured he would be found somewhere, having had an accident or been attacked by wild mountain animals and eaten.

CHAPTER 3

JESSIE WAS A TALL (FIVE FOOT TEN) WOMAN WITH BEAUTI-ful, naturally blond hair and huge dimples that automatically endeared her to nearly every person she met (only 20 to 30 percent of humans have dimples, which are often viewed as signs of natural beauty). She and John were the same age.

Sarah was raised in a small town fifty miles north of Mexico Beach named Blountstown. Her father was a wealthy landowner, and her mother hailed from Atlantathe daughter of rich real estate developers. Although she was an attractive woman, Sarah lacked the beauty of her sister-in-law; however, she possessed a winsome personality that everyone fell in love with almost immediately.

The wives had plans for their husbands. They married tall, handsome, smart men and wanted to enjoy the lives their mothers had lived. They were aware of the desire their husbands had to own and operate a new restaurant because the men had recently revisited the idea just before their parents' tragic accident. They now had the money to make their dream a reality.

Greg, the CPA, suggested that he, his brother, and their wives meet to discuss how to pursue their plan. He pointed out that it would take roughly $1 million to get the restaurant open for business. This included purchasing the lot, which John was fairly certain they could get for $260,000, rather than his employer's asking price of $295,000.

Preparing the lot; obtaining licenses and permits; and paying for architectural fees, restaurant equipment purchases, construction costs, insurance, and advertising expenses were projected at another $700,000 in Greg's pro forma statements. This would nearly consume the life insurance money, but they would basically be opening the restaurant debt free. Greg told John, Sarah, and Jessie that he was not recommending this approach because it would leave them no money for operating costs. He recommended that they use $200,000 of the insurance proceeds to get them all out of debt. Greg and John still had outstanding student loan balances, along with some credit card debt and auto loans.

He explained that being debt free would be more favorable to a bank. They would approach the three local banks with their pro forma statement and attempt to borrow $350,000 to fill the gap left after paying off existing debt, plus provide money for initial operating expenses. Greg and John would pledge the house their parents had left them as collateral for the loan. It had recently appraised for $365,000. All three banks were willing to loan the money, as well as provide a $200,000 line of credit. Greg and John decided to go with the bank their father had used for many years.

It was now July of 1996, and they wanted to be open no later than May 1, 1997. The contractors assured them ten months was enough time to meet their deadline so they would not miss the beginning of tourist season.

CHAPTER 4

AFTER CLOSING ON THE LOAN, THE COUPLES BEGAN TO move forward. Greg decided to keep his job with the CPA firm, while John and their two wives managed the day-to-day operations. Greg would handle all the tax and accounting issues after his normal work hours.

Seating capacity would initially be two hundred, with room to expand if successful. They would build a covered porch area, complete with outdoor tables, to accommodate those who chose to eat outside. This area would house one of two bars for people to enjoy drinks before, during, or after their meals and take in the beautiful sunsets over the gulf.

They now had to agree on a name for the restaurant. They had discussed several but finally settled upon the Red Lantern Bar and Grille. The name came from the red lantern the boys' grandfather had when they were kids. He used to tell them scary stories when they went camping, and the light from the red Coleman lantern was all the light he used. The boys had loved it.

During the planning phase, the wives thought it a good idea to construct a large stone fireplace at one end of the dining area, where they would mount one full-size, battery-operated red lantern. This would symbolize their husbands' grandfather's presence, as would be explained in flyers printed and placed on tables for people to read while they waited on their meals.

Once a month, on Saturday evening, either John or Greg would offer to tell some of the spooky stories they'd heard from their grandfather to the children in the restaurant, provided the parents agreed. The start of the storytelling session would always begin with turning on the lone red lantern and lowering the lights.

Sarah and Jessie placed ads for a chef online and with numerous restaurant magazines and employment agencies. They agreed an out-of-town chef would increase the restaurant's appeal and serve to minimize any preconceived ideas that might result from hiring a local.

Chef Meg LeBlanc was the person who caught their attention. Miss LeBlanc was forty-two years old, had never married, and had no children. She was born in New Orleans and had graduated from the prestigious Culinary Institute of America (CIA). From their research, they knew this college was the first to teach culinary arts in the United States and had graduated many successful certified master chefs. Sarah and Jessie considered her lack of a husband or family to be a plus and assumed she was probably a workaholic.

She passed a phone interview with flying colors. Meg explained that all she ever wanted to be was a chef, and she'd worked hard to establish herself as one. She had worked in several well-known restaurants in New Orleans and said she no longer enjoyed the hustle and bustle of her native city and wanted a fresh start in a much more relaxed community. It seemed exactly what she wanted at this point in her life.

It was December 1996 when the couples interviewed and hired Meg on the spot, agreeing to pay all her moving and travel expenses if she could start on April 1, 1997. They offered her a first-year salary of $75,000 with a promise of annual raises tied to the amount of net profit realized by the restaurant. She accepted without hesitating and thanked the Hugheses for placing confidence in her. She promised they would not be disappointed.

CHAPTER 5

THE BEACHES THAT STRETCHED FROM PANAMA CITY
Beach, Florida, to Biloxi, Mississippi, began to see significant development during the 2000s. The mom-and-pop hotels that had occupied the area were sold off to large development companies, which leveled the old hotels and started building high-rises, luxury condos, golf courses, and high-end restaurants. Mexico Beach also grew during this period but escaped the notice of the big-time developers.

The 250-mile distance along the gulf began to be referred to as "the Redneck Riviera," where many good ole boys vacationed and owned properties where they and their families enjoyed the crystal-clear emerald-green waters of the gulf, with its snow-white sandy beaches.

Along with all the development, the area attracted an "underworld element," filled with greed to profit from the illegal drug demand, prostitution rings, and untaxed moonshine that was available in almost any bar or restaurant if you knew whom to ask. The two families who controlled the illegal activity came to be known as "the Dixie Mafia" and were outreaches of two of the most notorious crime families in New York City. (They were referred to as simply "the Family," as people who knew and mentioned their names sometimes disappeared.)

The territory was divided into two separate areas: one stretching from Panama City Beach to Pensacola, Florida, and the other from Pensacola to Biloxi, Mississippi, where gambling had been legalized. The Family respected each other's geographic boundaries so as not to cause turf wars, which would inevitably bring unwanted attention to their organized crime operations.

As the Redneck Riviera developed, the Family enjoyed lucrative operations. They were making so much money, and they sometimes created legitimate businesses to launder it. This required bribing political officials who owned properties along the coast and had a vested interest to see the area continue growing. Although neither John nor Greg had any interactions with the Family at this time, they were aware of the existence of the organization.

Chef Meg LeBlanc arrived for her first day of work on April 1, 1997, as agreed. Greg, John, and their wives were told everything was on schedule for the May 1 grand opening. Sarah and Jessie explained to Meg that the hiring of staff would be her decision, provided she stayed within the strict budget Greg had prepared. In addition, Chef LeBlanc would be responsible for developing the menu. To have everything in place by May 1, Meg worked tirelessly in finding, hiring, and training the staff, as well as establishing a menu she believed would be well received by the restaurant patrons.

She relished the idea of being able to purchase fresh fruits and vegetables just a few miles up the road during the summer months. John agreed to make the daily purchases according to her directions. The hours of operation were to be six days weekly (Tuesday through Sunday) from 4:00 to 10:00 p.m. This would allow customers the option of dining early or late.

On Thursday morning, May 1, 1997, the chamber of commerce held a ribbon-cutting ceremony at 11:00 a.m. to officially open the new restaurant. All the chamber members were present, along with a number of locals congratulating the Hugheses and wishing them success.

Chef LeBlanc's menu choices had been printed and distributed in the community, as well as posted online on their website two weeks prior to the grand opening. The locals' mouths were watering by opening day. By 3:30 p.m. on Friday, May 2, a line of hungry people had gathered to be among some of the first to try the new restaurant. The Hugheses, Chef LeBlanc, and the staff were ecstatic to remain nearly full all night.

After several years in business, the Red Lantern Bar and Grille was so successful that two of the other local restaurants closed their doors due to the lack of customers. They couldn't compete with the Hughes family.

Sarah and Jessie could not have been happier, now that they were able to live the affluent lives their mothers had enjoyed. They had plans for homes that were nice but not considered extravagant.

It was now 2007, and Mexico Beach's population had increased 15 percent in the past ten years. It was still a small community but large enough that its residents did not know everyone in town.

The construction boom in Panama City Beach was in full swing. As the hotels and condos went up, so did tourism and crime. Some of the new residents of Mexico Beach were people fed up with the traffic, overpriced housing market, and increase in violent crime in the western part of the county; they had moved to the beach on the extreme eastern border of Bay County. They were attracted by the smaller community; the beautiful beaches, with plenty of public access; and the lower cost of living.

The first year went well enough that the Hugheses did not have to draw on their line of credit, but they kept it in place as a safety net. Greg maintained his job at his dad's old CPA firm, and John, Sarah, and Jessie worked hard to build and maintain the restaurant's reputation.

It took four years to pay off the bank loan. At the end of the fifth year, the Red Lantern Bar and Grille enjoyed gross sales of $4.6 million and netted a respectable 11 percent profit, or $506,000, which the Hugheses shared equally. At this point, Greg left the CPA firm and devoted his efforts full time to helping the others.

They all agreed hiring Chef Meg LeBlanc was the *best* decision they made. She was not only an excellent chef but also managed the staff members so well that none had quit during the five-year period. John remembered their dad saying, "Treat the staff well, and they will serve you well, no matter what business you are in."

Meg LeBlanc's salary had increased from $75,000 to $95,000 in five years. She loved living in Mexico Beach but believed she should be making more, as it was her culinary expertise that had put the restaurant on the map. She had trained a very good staff and was now assisted by two young cooks. Although Meg considered herself happy, she wanted more. She had just turned forty-seven and didn't want to have to continue this type of work for ten to twenty more years.

CHAPTER 6

STEPHEN SADLER, OWNER OF THE MEXICO BEACH FUNERAL
Home and a college friend of Greg Hughes, was a regular at
the Red Lantern Bar and Grille. He often dropped by to have
a few drinks and a good meal and visit his old friend. His
wife, Leticia, rarely joined him because she did not want to
encourage his drinking. She detested it and was concerned
that it might become the source of the failure of his business
and their marriage.

Late one evening, after the restaurant had closed, Greg
and Stephen sat in Greg's office drinking. They reminisced
about their college years. Stephen lamented that his business
was not doing well, and Greg offered some expert advice. He
suggested Stephen add a crematory to the operation. Stephen mulled over his suggestion for a few minutes, then said,
"Yeah, I've thought about that, but where am I going to get
the money? The bank will not likely lend it because of my
declining financials."

Greg responded that he would lend the money. Stephen asked, "You'd do that for me?"

Greg said, "Of course I will, my old friend."

They shook hands on the deal, and he made plans to add the crematory to the funeral home. The two continued talking for a while, but Greg began to cry. Stephen asked, "What's the matter?"

Greg said, in his drunken state, "I killed my grandfather." Stephen asked, "*What?*"

Greg replied, "I killed my grandfather in 1981 because he was a piece of crap."

Greg cupped his face in both hands and sobbed with remorse over what he had done. He looked at Stephen and said, "You must promise to never repeat what I just told you; only John and Dad knew about it."

Stephen asked, "John knew?"

Greg answered, "*Yes*, he helped me dispose of the body."

They knew the statute of limitations did not apply to murder and they could still be prosecuted.

Meg LeBlanc was an attractive, friendly person and an accomplished chef who was admired by many of the townspeople. The residents knew her and had great respect for her accomplishments. Stephen was one of her admirers. He enjoyed conversations with her at the restaurant, where she sometimes doubled as the bartender. Stephen found her very attractive and loved to listen to her stories about growing up in New Orleans. Meg also found the forty-year-old with his salt-and-pepper hair and medium build attractive. Although she had met Leticia a few times, Meg thought it strange his wife rarely joined him at the restaurant and concluded the marriage was likely weak.

Late one evening, Stephen offered to walk her to her car after the restaurant closed. When they arrived at her vehicle, he embraced and kissed her passionately. Meg asked if he would like to follow her home and have a drink. He jumped at the opportunity.

When they arrived, Meg offered something to eat, but Stephen declined, saying he had eaten at the restaurant a few hours earlier. Meg made his favorite drink, Diet Coke and Gentleman Jack, then excused herself to freshen up and changed into a lovely nightgown. She returned with two lines of cocaine spread evenly over a glass tray and suggested they snort it to "rev" them up for a night of passion. Stephen was not a drug user but had smoked pot while in college. He agreed to participate—after all, he thought he probably needed a stimulant to keep up with her.

As they sat talking, Meg asked if he thought this was a good idea. Stephen told her his marriage had been "on the rocks" for years, and the only reason he and Leticia remained married was they believed divorce would create a stigma neither wanted to endure. He asked Meg why she had never married. She explained she was more interested in a career as a chef in her younger days and chose to remain single to pursue it without the responsibilities of being a wife. They had begun kissing when Meg asked if he would stay the night. He said his wife was out of town, so she led him to the bedroom.

As Stephen prepared to leave for work the next morning, Meg asked, "Where do we go from here?"

He replied, "I don't know but hope I can continue to see you in the foreseeable future. But, Meg, please don't mention our night together to anyone, as the last thing I need on my plate is a divorce." Meg nodded that she understood.

He arrived at the funeral home, where his secretary informed him that the sheriff had left a message, asking that he return the call ASAP. He called the sheriff, who asked that he meet him at the county morgue, where two unidentified bodies were awaiting autopsies. Stephen told his secretary where he was going. She stated, "You seem awfully chipper this morning."

He replied, saying he had had a great night playing Texas Hold'em with his buddies. She laughed, asking if he had won. He said, "Yeah, you might say I got lucky" and headed out the door.

When he arrived at the morgue, he and the sheriff entered the exam room, where two Caucasian males were laying on the exam tables. The sheriff said they had been found in a dumpster in Panama City Beach early that morning. His deputies said neither had any form of identification. After performing the autopsies, he concluded the cause and approximate time of death to be asphyxiation occurring between 11:00 and 11:45 p.m. the previous night.

The sheriff notified the press, and coverage of the story ran on the evening news channel, WJHG, asking viewers with any information to please contact the sheriff's office. A week passed, and no one came forward with anything. Toxicology tests were performed. Fingerprints and DNA samples were removed from the corpses and ran through the Integrated Automated Fingerprint Identification System (IAFIS) and the Federal DNA Database Unit (FDDU) maintained by the FBI to identify the two men. Nothing turned up.

Stephen had a contract with Bay County that paid him a fee to cremate unidentified bodies. It certainly wasn't a lucrative one, but at least it provided some much-needed business and prevented the county from expending larger sums to bury the unknowns in the county's paupers' graveyard.

This was the third time in eight months that unidentifiable bodies had turned up in one of the Family's territories, and the sheriff became suspicious the murders were linked to the organized crime families because the murders were "professional"—no evidence left behind and no identification found on the victims. The only common thread was the victims had used illegal drugs shortly before their deaths. Stephen chalked the murders up to drug deals gone bad, and the sheriff tended to agree.

CHAPTER 7

OVER A MATTER OF A FEW MONTHS, STEPHEN'S LIFE HAD become very complicated. His drinking habit had begun to spiral out of control, his business was in trouble, he was behind in payments to his best friend for the crematory, his marriage was falling apart, he now knew about the murdered grandfather, and he was involved in an affair with Meg, who he thought might be a cocaine addict. He wondered how he had managed to make such a mess of his life.

While exchanging pillow talk with Meg one night, Stephen confided that his life was falling apart. He told her everything seemed to keep going wrong, with the exception of her. She was the only bright spot. He was falling in love with Meg and even shared Greg's secret with her. He told Meg he had to find a way to lift some of his burdens, and soon.

The two began using cocaine more frequently. Stephen said he thought it helped to energize him and increase his concentration level when, in fact, he was only digging his hole deeper.

Meg's dealer was in Panama City Beach, and she met him there about once a month to resupply. When Stephen questioned her about where she got the cocaine, she told him not to worry, that she had an out-of-town supplier. He let it go, not really caring one way or another.

Meg's supplier was one of the underbosses of the Family's eastern territory. She usually met Tony (that was the name he used, although she was sure it was not his real name) at one of his strip clubs, where she would appear to be just another business associate. He boasted about his ownership of two strip clubs, a meat-processing plant, a linen business, and several fast-food restaurants. Meg liked him, and he liked her. He was always well dressed, polite, and quite the gentleman with her.

Tony had hoped that over time, she might consider a relationship. She did not, explaining she was involved in a successful relationship and thought it unwise to mix business with pleasure anyway. He accepted her answer but always considered her a "possibility."

For ten consecutive years, the Red Lantern Bar and Grille enjoyed success, and its owners felt life was good. Both brothers had completed their new homes on the beach, and their wives couldn't have been happier.

It was 2007, and the Great Recession in the United States was about to hit. The country had seen no greater recession since the Great Depression of the 1930s. From December 2007 to June 2009, the country endured the worst recession in nearly ninety years. The Red Lantern Bar and Grille did not escape. During the nineteen-month period, sales dropped 35 percent, and Greg became gravely alarmed. He suggested drawing on their line of credit, which they had never done, in an attempt to weather the financial storm. His partners agreed.

By early 2009, the Hugheses' business was struggling. Rising costs and declining customers had reduced the sales and, thus, their profit margin. Greg and John were now strapped with new mortgages and a tapped-out line of credit, and Stephen had begun to miss his monthly payments for the financing of the crematory, further straining Greg's cash flow.

The Hughes brothers had to cut costs. They needed to make decisions about laying off staff members to reduce overhead. This was a painstaking task, as many of the staff had been with them since opening day. The brothers also had to find a new meat supplier, as the company they had used in nearby Apalachicola had closed its doors for good.

For the first time, Greg and John included Meg LeBlanc in reviewing the corporate books, hoping she could contribute suggestions for ways to reduce costs without sacrificing quality. Meg proved very helpful and assisted the brothers with a plan to reduce supply costs; however, while reviewing the books, she was angered by the amount of money the Hugheses had been making. She had not received a raise in the past two years, nor had any of the staff, while the Hugheses had built new homes.

Meanwhile, corpses continued to roll into the morgue. Although the sheriff had begun to identify some through fingerprinting and DNA sampling, none of the murders had been solved. A clear motive had never been established, and no evidence was ever found linking the murders to anyone.

Greg found a Panama City Beach meat-processing plant online to replace his previous supplier. Although the prices were higher, he believed he had no choice but to buy from the company. The plant was owned by Tony. Greg and John met with him and hammered out the details of the cuts of meat and quantities they would buy. The contract stipulated the brothers could order small quantities on an as-needed basis, deliverable within forty-eight hours to their restaurant, with payment terms being net thirty days. They considered it a normal business transaction, having no clue about "Tony's" real identity.

Tony also did not know Meg LeBlanc was the chef at the Red Lantern Bar and Grille, as he and she never discussed it; they had no reason to. As far as Tony was concerned, he was only interested in a relationship with her. Four months into the contract, Greg and John began to lag in the timeliness of their payments to Tony's company. He decided to pay the brothers a visit to address the issue.

CHAPTER 8

DURING ONE OF MEG'S "SLEEPOVER PARTIES," SHE ASKED Stephen if he was certain Greg's story of the murder of his grandfather, and John being his accomplice, was true. Stephen replied, *yes*. He thought it was because he knew his friend well and could tell how upset Greg became while telling him. Then he asked Meg why she cared. She answered, "While reviewing the corporate books, I became aware of how much they are raking in at the expense of their staff." She told Stephen how angry it made her and vowed to "make them pay." Stephen asked, "And just how do you plan to do that, my love?"

Meg told him her plan to use the knowledge of the grandfather's murder to demand $100,000 in cash, which she viewed as "back pay." Stephen replied that Greg would know he had told Meg about the murder, but that he didn't care because he no longer cared for them.

Stephen plotted with Meg to also use their knowledge to force Greg to forgive the remaining balance of his loan. The two believed there was no way Greg or John would contest them since they could both still be prosecuted.

Meg arrived to work the next day and asked if she could meet with Greg and John alone. They agreed and were startled by her demands. After their initial shock, Greg asked why she wanted Stephen's loan forgiven. He asked if they were having an affair. She told him they were, saying, "I love Stephen and he loves me."

Greg denied ever saying such a thing. He explained that he and Stephen had been drinking heavily one night and Greg broke down crying, remembering the disappearance of his grandfather, who was never found. He told Meg he did not murder his grandfather. And he asked her, furthermore, how she could believe he and John were capable of such a thing. Greg fired Meg on the spot, knowing he had two well-trained cooks who could prepare all of Meg's dishes. She stormed out of the office, furious! They immediately called the cooks to their office, explained they had just fired Meg, and offered substantial raises to stay on board. The cooks gladly agreed.

Meg called Stephen and told him what had happened. After a few moments of complete silence, Stephen exclaimed, "Oh no!"

Shortly afterward, Greg called Stephen, asking, "How could you? After all I've done for you, how could you accuse me of such a thing?"

Stephen replied, "That's what you told me."

Greg said, "*No*, you completely misunderstood me that night. You need to get away from that woman and come to your senses, and by the way, I know about your affair. If you don't break if off with Meg, I am going to tell Leticia." He then hung up, slamming the phone down.

Meg LaBlanc decided on a plan to get even with the Hugheses. First, she called the Franklin, North Carolina sheriff's office to confirm the 1981 death of the grandfather. She was told the old files stated the man disappeared and was never found so presumed dead. In Meg's mind, this was enough to confirm Greg's statement to Stephen.

She called Letitia Sadler and told her about Greg's admission of murder and John being his accomplice, and that their wives knew nothing about it. Leticia asked, "Why are you telling me this?" Meg answered, "Because I think Sarah and Jessie deserve to know what kind of men they married, and they would never believe *me* if I told them, plus your husband is the person Greg told."

When Stephen arrived home from work, Leticia told him about Meg's phone call. She asked him, "Is she telling the truth?" Stephen replied, "That's what Greg told me," then suggested she make the call to Sarah and Jessie. Leticia asked, "How does Meg know Greg said this to you?" Stephen answered, "Because one night, I told her at the Red Lantern." Leticia asked, "If it is true, why would you tell Meg?" Stephen hesitated, thinking about Greg's threat to tell Leticia of his affair, then answered, "Please sit down, Letitia. I have something to explain."

After Stephen explained his affair to her, she began crying and then told him to expect divorce papers soon. She said to him, "Pack your things and get out!" Stephen moved into his funeral home.

Leticia then made the phone call to Sarah and Jessie and told them what Meg claimed. Neither believed a word of it until Leticia explained Stephen and Meg had been having an affair and that Stephen confirmed Greg's admission. She also added what Meg was told by the Franklin sheriff's office.

After Sarah and Jessie learned of Meg's firing, they asked their husbands what happened. Greg and John explained they caught Meg skimming cash from the bar registers. Sarah asked the brothers, "Did this have anything to do with the murder of your grandfather?" John replied, "Our grandfather just disappeared. There was no evidence he was murdered. Why would you think he was murdered?" Jessie screamed, "Stop lying, tell the truth!"

Sarah and Jessie told the brothers about Leticia's phone conversation with Meg. Jessie asked, "Did you two murder your grandfather?" Greg explained everything, saying he was overcome with rage about his grandmother's needless death and his grandfather's abusiveness. He said, "I was overcome with anger and hatred, and now John and I have to live with it." Sarah replied, "Yeah, and Jessie and I have to also," then asked, "Have you idiots told anyone besides the Sadlers and Meg?" Greg answered, "No, and I actually only told Stephen. He told Meg, and she told Leticia to get revenge on us for firing her. "Sarah," Greg said, "Meg tried to blackmail us for one hundred thousand dollars. We denied everything, then fired her." Sarah said, "I'm not going back to the life we lived before the Red Lantern; all we have to do is figure out how to deal with the Sadlers and Meg." Jessie said, "Leave that up to me."

CHAPTER 9

THAT EVENING, TONY SHOWED UP AT THE RESTAURANT with two of his "enforcers." They all proceeded to Greg's office, where John offered them a drink. Tony declined, saying he was there on business. He explained that they were forty-five days delinquent in their payment on a $15,000 balance and asked how they planned to resolve the matter. John immediately responded that payment in full would be made by the end of the week. Tony said, "If I don't have my money in twenty-four hours, some very bad things are about to happen." When John asked if he was threatening them, Tony replied, "Just have my money," then left. Greg and John were concerned about Tony. They agreed to take the $15,000 they owed him from the reserve operating fund and deliver the money the next morning.

As they exited, they bumped into Meg in the lobby, who had returned to clear out her personal items. Tony recognized her immediately and asked why she was there. She told him that up until a few hours ago, she had been the head chef but was fired. Tony said he was sorry to hear that; then she asked if she could meet with him the next day. Tony agreed, thinking he may have an opportunity to help her and worm his way into a relationship.

When Greg and John arrived at Tony's office the next morning, they paid the debt in full and then asked if they could continue doing business with him. Tony answered with a resounding *no* and told them to get out of his office. He explained that their relationship was terminated effective immediately.

On their drive back, Greg and John discussed what to do. Again, they found themselves with no meat supplier and would likely be unable to secure a replacement as quickly as they needed one.

It had been weeks since Greg had spoken with Stephen about his and Meg's plot to blackmail him. Stephen had stopped coming to the restaurant, and Greg became concerned about what was becoming of his old friend. He decided to pay him a visit.

When he arrived at the funeral home, Stephen was seated at his desk and asked why he bothered to stop by. Greg said, "I just wanted to check to see how you were doing."

Stephen responded that he was doing better. He had broken off the affair with Meg, telling her he had to get his life in order. He'd told his wife about the affair, asking she forgive him. He had completely stopped drinking and using drugs but now had to live in the funeral home and deal with divorce. Greg said to Stephen, "I know about the divorce and every-thing else, but now Sarah and Jessie halfway believe me and John murdered our grandfather because of your big mouth."

Greg asked him to catch up on his loan payments as soon as possible. Stephen said, "I'm doing the best I can. If I don't keep my business afloat, you will never see your money." Greg congratulated Stephen on the steps he had taken to straighten his life out, saying that those were all good decisions and he was certain things would work out if Stephen just stayed the course. Greg commented, "As for me and John, we lost our only meat supplier and are unsure what we are going to do." He asked Stephen if he had any bright ideas, to which Ste-phen answered no.

Meg met with Tony the same day Greg and John paid their debt off. As she entered his office, he greeted her with a big hug and kiss on the cheek, asking how she was doing. Meg said she was not sure what she was going to do since the Hughes brothers had fired her. Tony asked how he could help. She broke down and started to sob, saying, "They ruined my life and my relationship and now they are going to pay!" Tony sat beside her on the couch and consoled her with kind words. Meg said she had always liked Tony but didn't feel right about a relationship when, as she had explained, she was already in one.

Tony recalled their previous conversation about the mat-ter and said, "I really like your sense of loyalty."

She leaned over and kissed him passionately, then said, "I am ready for that relationship."

Tony then asked, "Why don't you and I go to the club, do a little partying, then go back to my hotel, where you can spend the night?" She answered that it was the best idea she had heard all day.

CHAPTER 10

STEPHEN HAD BEEN THINKING ABOUT GREG'S VISIT. HE WAS surprised his old friend was concerned enough to stop by to offer words of encouragement after all that had transpired with Meg. He was happy to be back on speaking terms with Greg.

In college, Stephen had read about ancient civilizations, some dating back to the early 1500s, found in the Amazon River Basin of South America. He was specifically intrigued by the Indian tribes that were found to be cannibalistic by the English explorers who traveled there to study the cultures.

One of the major causes of death among the tribes was starvation. Some had learned to supplement their limited food supply by eating their dead. Many believed the practice also allowed the spirits of their fellow tribe members to remain alive in those who ate them, providing them spiritual strength.

As recorded by the early English explorers, some of them had also eaten flesh to prevent their own starvation. They believed they had no choice. Their memoirs indicated how tasty it was after having been tenderized, smoked, and seasoned with herbs and spices readily available in the forest. They said it sure beat the slow, painful death of starvation.

In their notes, the explorers indicated that the Indians were meticulous at preparing the human flesh to be cooked and consumed. One common rule among them was to never eat the body of a person who had died in any way but naturally and to never eat the brain or entrails because that's where diseases resided; they only ate the flesh. They noticed, in comparing the cannibalistic tribes with others that did not practice cannibalism, that the cannibals lived longer, healthier lives and were far more robust in physical appearance.

Stephen understood that the Western world considered cannibalism a barbaric practice but found there were no laws specifically outlawing eating human flesh, per se, with the exception of Idaho. Most states, however, had laws that made it difficult to legally obtain and consume human remains. Idaho was the only state that explicitly discussed cannibalism in its legislation and prohibited the practice but did allow for it in cases of "extreme life-threatening conditions" as the only apparent means of survival. Although Stephen found the idea abhorrent, it triggered a thought.

Stephen rang Greg and asked if he remembered asking if he had any "bright ideas" as to how to address Greg and John's problem of quickly securing a new meat supplier. Greg said he remembered, then asked, "Why?" Stephen asked him to meet him at the funeral home that night. Greg agreed.

As Stephen explained the steady flow of corpses coming to him from the county morgue and the increase in regular cremation business, he suggested using the human flesh in the restaurant. Stephen said there would be no cost to the Hughes brothers if Greg agreed to let the "free meat" satisfy the balance of Stephen's loan to him. Greg burst into laughter, saying, "You must be joking."

Stephen said he was *not*. All he was suggesting was using the human flesh as an interim solution to buy time for them to secure a new meat supplier. Stephen said he had learned some of the ancient techniques for preparing human flesh from books he'd studied on cannibalism in the Amazon. Many of the Indian tribes had perfected the process, and some of the Amazonian explorers had noted how tasty it was, he told Greg.

He said he would prepare the flesh in his funeral home, where he would wrap it in ordinary meat packing paper and then incinerate what was left over. The families of the deceased would never know the difference because they would be provided urns containing the ashes of the bones and entrails, just like any ordinary cremation. Stephen could see the expression on Greg's face change from disbelief to real possibility. Greg joked, "Yeah, I could change the menu choice for a porterhouse to 'rump roast.'" They laughed hysterically.

Greg explained the plan to his brother, who reluctantly agreed, knowing they had little choice if they wanted to remain in business. John instructed the cooks how to tenderize and season the meat per Stephen's instructions. The two cooks grilled some of the meat, ate it, and commented on the superb quality and savory taste. One commented, "Now that's a meal people would die for."

After two months, Greg was able to enter a contract with a new supplier located in the nearby town of Chipley, Florida. The Red Lantern Bar and Grille had survived the Great Recession, which ended in June 2009. They were back on their feet.

CHAPTER 11

MEG LEBLANC MOVED TO PANAMA CITY BEACH WITH TONY.
After he determined she was basically a cocaine addict and alcoholic, subject to fits of uncontrollable anger, he arrived at the conclusion that she posed a potential risk to the Family's operations.

Meg LeBlanc's body was found in a dumpster near the Panama City Beach Walmart, asphyxiated, with her face disfigured to the point that she was unidentifiable. WJHG carried the story, asking anyone with any information to report it to the county sheriff. No one ever did, and Stephen cremated the body.

Stephen's wife filed for divorce and moved back to California to live with her mother. He was distraught and knew it was all his fault. Although Stephen's business was now profitable and his loan to Greg paid in full, he was depressed over the things he had done. On November 3, 2009, he hung himself in the crematory, thinking his life was no longer worth living.

The Amazonian cannibals fiercely believed that the spirits of bodies that died violently should never be eaten. The spirits were believed to live among the living until their deaths were avenged. Although Greg, John, and Stephen had never eaten any flesh, they were all responsible for the desecration of human bodies, causing others to eat them.

The Hughes brothers continued telling their monthly stories on Saturday nights to the children and frequently found the lone red Coleman lantern glowing mysteriously after it had been turned off for hours. They believed their grandfather's spirit still lived among them.

The Red Lantern Bar and Grille resumed prospering, although it took months to overcome the recession. The Hughes family moved forward as though nothing had ever happened.

Two years later, Greg was hospitalized for days with a mysterious infection before eventually dying. He suffered from night sweats, excruciating abdominal pain, a fever of unknown origin, and hallucinations. The physicians were unable to diagnose or cure his illness, saying they had never seen anything like it. As John watched his brother die an unmerciful death, he remembered what Stephen had said about the Indian tribe's unwillingness to eat flesh from a body that had died violently.

John would never forget what his brother said with his last breath. He leaned over the hospital bed to hear Greg whisper, "*You're next.*"

42

9 798822 963498